I0788093

A Trip With

God

(A Psychedelic Viewpoint of Religion)

John Powers

Published by: Book Writing Solution
www.bookwritingsolution.com

DEDICATION

This book is dedicated to the psychedelic
community.

TABLE OF CONTENTS

Dedication iii

Prologue vi

Chapter 1: Questions 1

Chapter 2: What Were They Eating 10

Chapter 3: The Search 33

Chapter 4: A New Guy In Town 42

Chapter 5: Godhead................................... 58

Chapter 6: Freedom 70

Chapter 7: The "Wow" Factor 79

Chapter 8: Brain Power 89

Chapter 9: Try Some Of This................. 100

Chapter 10: Soul Food 106

Chapter 11: Answers? 115

About The Author 133

PROLOGUE

People have experienced events in their lives that pointed them in many different directions, paths, vocations, careers and beliefs. Born and raised a Catholic, my religion was as much a part of my life as breakfast, lunch and dinner. I partied with friends, dated girls in high school, worked, exercised, and was as normal a kid as any.

I got drafted into the Army and went to Vietnam, which was my first wake-up call. I was a twenty-year-old naive kid when I went to Vietnam, and when I got back home after a year in the war, I wasn't a naive kid anymore. Most of my friends were deep in the drug culture of the late 1960s, and I fell right in with them. That was when I took my first dose of LSD, the second wake-up call in my life. That is also when the questions about religion and life itself changed me forever.

CHAPTER 1
QUESTIONS

There are some questions I've been asking myself for years. After some frightening, life-threatening experiences, I began questioning things that were instilled in me from my youth about my Catholic upbringing and God. I was taught that if I believe in God, I'll "go to Heaven" when I die, and if I was a good Catholic, God would protect me.

Psychedelics changed all that for me. Baptism, communion, confirmation, confession, and all the ritual that comes with being a good Catholic are all part of this structured religion I started questioning years ago. Being thrown into a war, almost drowning from defective scuba gear, motorcycle accidents, and other near-death experiences that have happened to me in my years on earth are experiences that God saved me from dying, according to the Catholic faith.

Was God protecting me, or were these experiences just part of what's called life? In the Catholic religion, it is believed that you are born with "original sin." Baptism washes away this original sin, so you must be baptized soon after birth. This allows you entry into the Catholic Church, free of sin. If you die with sin on your soul, you'll "go to Hell." You can repent by confessing these sins to a priest in a booth, in a church. He'll give you prayers to say based on the quantity and severity of your sins, and your sins will be forgiven. "What"! This means I can sin all I want, and if I confess these sins to a priest, I'll be absolved. My sins will be eliminated from my soul, and I can die with peace of mind knowing I'm going to Heaven. This is a tenet of the Catholic Church. I'm not disparaging people who believe in the Catholic way, I am questioning it.

In approximately 320 AD, a hierarchy was established in the Christian church. Priests, Bishops, the Pope, the most revered bishop of the Catholic hierarchy, is the chain of command leading one to the most holy, Jesus Christ. This is similar to a military structure. A question I often ask is, if I believe in the "Word" of Jesus, why can't I go right to the top and connect with Jesus directly? What makes this hierarchy so important? If I believe in Jesus's "Word", the same as this clergy does, what makes them the pathway to God?

I understand that these people are to be revered by the believers in the Catholic Church and that they dedicate their lives to their religion, but why can't a person live a good, wholesome, moral, Christian life without having to go to church and revere the hierarchy of the church? This is the Protestant or Lutheran point of view. Both are Christian, but neither sees eye to eye. Church is a communal organization where people gather to worship. But what if one wants to live a good, moral life without going to church, synagogue, or mosque? Does that make him or her less of a good moral person?

After Jesus died, people who believed in his "word" gathered in seclusion to continue Christ's teachings. They were persecuted if they were caught discussing His teachings by the existing Roman government. The governing elites didn't want people to believe in a higher and more sacred power than theirs, similar to some governments of today. In most countries today, laws have been passed to separate the church and the state, allowing people to freely practice religion without government interference if they so choose. It took approximately three hundred and twenty years after Jesus death before Christianity was officially recognized in the Roman Empire by the ruler Constantine who declared Christianity the official religion of Rome. There was no hierarchy in the years prior to Constantine's' decree. Although the Apostles and other disciples were revered, there was no official structured hierarchy. There were the believers and the nonbelievers. These enlightened believers, who had secret meetings in caves and met secretly in their homes, took their lives into their hands by promoting Christian teachings that lasted over two thousand years. They met, discussed things that brought them to spiritual heights, and supped together as if emulating the "last supper." Exactly what they ate and drank at these gatherings is not known. What is known is that they "broke bread" and drank wine and beer, "spirits." The bread was called manna; in the Bible, it is referred to as "manna from heaven." When I hear of "manna from heaven" or "spirits" (wine and beer), I wonder if this manna and this wine and beer had something to do with their spiritual awakenings. Did manna come from heaven, or did manna open heaven's door? Were these consumables psychoactive due to ergot-infected mold on wheat, barley and rye from which bread, manna, was made?

Where is heaven, where is hell, where is God? Why did Constantine only allow four Gospels in the Bible if there were twelve Apostles? My interest in these and other mysteries was piqued in the late sixties and early seventies when I dabbled in psychoactive substances and became more interested in the spiritual world of early Christianity, Buddhism, Hinduism and other spiritual realms. In reading about cultures that used different substances to "commune" with God, I learned things about these cultures and their use of natural hallucinogens in their spiritual ceremonies.

It was very interesting that there was a commonality in most of these cultures: the way to "enlightenment" through something they ate, drank or smoked. American Indians used peyote and smoked "peace pipes" to commune with the "Great Spirit." Many Mexican cultures use mescaline, peyote and other psychoactive plants to commune with God. Amazonian cultures use ayahuasca and other psychoactive plant substances in their quest to commune with God. Who is to say that thousands of years ago, Jesus and his followers didn't ingest some kind of mind-altering substance, for instance, "manna from heaven," intentionally or unintentionally, to light the Divine spark within and "commune" with God the Father? In the Christian religion receiving communion, the Eucharist, is the most holy part of the mass. It is the part of the mass when you "commune" with God. Most communion takers go to the altar, receive a wafer, or host, which simulates the body of Christ, then go back to their pew, say a prayer of forgiveness, and that's it; they have "received communion." But do these communion takers ever stop to think that Jesus and the Apostles might have been eating and drinking something that actually made them "commune" with God, as do other cultures that eat and drink things in their ceremonies to commune with their God? I believe there are many ways to commune with God, and ingesting certain psychoactive substances is surely one of them.

Fifteen hundred years before Jesus, people trekked to a place called Eleusis in Greece to discover the "Mysteries of Eleusis." When they left Eleusis, they were "enlightened." No one knows for sure what happened there. Hence the "mysteries," but people went there annually and left in a different state of mind. It is believed that this annual trek to Eleusis was to commune with God. It was a spiritual journey. Something happened to them there that "enlightened" them. It is speculated that they ate and drank things that took them over the spiritual threshold to "see the light" and commune with God.

A drink called kykeon, it was discovered, was drunk there and is believed to have been the elixir that opened their God eyes. Let's remember that in those days, food and drink were crudely made. Beer and wine in those days weren't like the beer and wine of today. This practice of trekking to Eleusis lasted until about 500 AD when Christian elites put a stop to it. It was part of the "believe in Christianity or die" edict. Communion in Jesus's days may have been different than today's communion. Those who have experimented with psychoactive substances in modern times can vouch for the spiritual connection, the "communion" with God, that psychedelics provides. Psychedelics can answer some of the questions about who, where and what God is.

CHAPTER 2
WHAT WERE THEY EATING

M any cultures believe in the "rite of passage." This is the experience of passing over a threshold from a spiritually unaware life to an aware, or more enlightened, spiritual life. One becomes a man from a boy, a woman from a girl, a mature from an immature person, in the hope that he or she will take life more seriously and start living a more virtuous life, a step into adulthood. In the Catholic Religion, First Holy Communion and Conformation are the stepping stones, the "rites of passage," into the Catholic Church. Bar Mitzvah and Bat Mitzvah are the Jewish "rites of passage."

Mexican Indians and American Indians use psychoactive substances, peyote, for example, for their "rite of passage," and other cultures use substances to cross over the threshold into this new, more spiritual, adult life. You might say they are being "born again." You leave your past life and become a new person. This "born again" event can happen anytime in a person's life. Most governments deplore the use of psychoactive substances because the results of these mind-expanding substances awaken people to a more skeptical view of authority. The authority of government becomes second to the authority of a higher power, namely God.

The 1960s and 1970s antigovernment counter-culture movement is an example of this awakening to authority. Mind-altering drugs were pervasive in the 1960s and 70s, so the government simply made these substances illegal (The Controlled Substances Act, 1970). Two thousand-plus years ago, there was no Food and Drug Administration. No one inspected the food people ate, or the drink they drank, to see if it was "fit" for consumption. Food and drink were valuable commodities, and people toiled daily to ensure that there was food on the table. It was so precious that it was rarely wasted. Sometimes food was eaten, and drink was drunk that had begun to spoil.

There were no preservatives, nothing to keep bread fresh or wine and beer from turning "bad" in those days. It was too valuable to throw out, so it was consumed. It's well known that when certain foods start to spoil, mold grows on them. Studies have found that some of these molds have medicinal characteristics, for example, penicillin, and have certain healing effects on people. Other studies have found that there are other effects, such as psychoactive reactions, when certain molds are ingested. One study that fascinates me is the study of ergot, a mold that grows on wheat, barley and rye, which is what beer and bread (manna) are made from. Ergot, it has been discovered, is the base ingredient of LSD. Strange, don't you think? Could ergot be the source of "manna from heaven," as the Bible mentions? Mycology is the study of mushrooms, and it has been discovered that certain mushrooms have a psychedelic effect on people.

When ergot or certain mushrooms are ingested, the effects on people are psychedelic. Many people who have eaten LSD or certain "magic mushrooms" curiously turn to spiritual life. When any psychedelic is eaten, the mind is expanded, which means parts of the brain become awakened or activated. Psychedelics have a mysterious effect on the mind, but it is definitely an effect that most people who have "tripped," especially more than a few times, will not forget. In most people, it awakens a spiritual quest. After the psychedelic experience, curiosity awakens in you. You begin to question things that didn't seem important to you prior to your psychedelic experience. You will start questioning things you previously knew about but never thought seriously about. You'll dig deeper into things that didn't seem important before your psychedelic trip. For many, a spiritual curiosity emerges.

In 1938 LSD was discovered while experimenting with ergot, the fungus that grows on wheat, rye and barley. Research was stopped and set aside until 1943 when the research was restarted. Albert Hofmann, a chemist working for Sandoz Pharmaceutical, while working on ergot research, unknowingly ingested this discovery. An hour or so later, on a bicycle trip back to his home, he started experiencing things, unlike anything he had ever experienced.

He was "tripping" on this chemical that he was working on and became curious as to how and why he felt and saw things this strange way. He realized it was this drug that he was experimenting with and had mistakenly ingested. His curiosity was piqued, and he continued experimenting with it. He was never the same afterwards. The spiritual door in his mind was opened. After a few more LSD experiences, his priorities about life changed. He left the corporate world and started looking into the world of spirituality in other cultures, especially South American cultures where mushrooms, mescaline and ayahuasca were used regularly in God-searching ceremonies. It is a common effect on people who use psychoactive substances to become more spiritually oriented.

Gordon Wasson, a New York banker, along with his Russian wife Tina, are the two people who popularized psychedelic mushrooms in America. In Russia, where Tina was from, the psychedelic effects of some mushrooms were well known, unlike in America, where psychedelics were not known. On their honeymoon in the Poconos, Tina found patches of these mushrooms and explained the effects of these mushrooms to Gordon. He became curious about these mushrooms. They traveled to Mexico to learn about the effects of psychoactive mushrooms in some Mexican cultures' spiritual ceremonies.

He experimented with them in a small Mexican town with the shaman Maria Sabina. His psychedelic experience while in Sabina's care changed his view of the world. Wasson returned to America and, along with Albert Hofmann, researched the chemical structure of these "magic mushrooms," a term he coined, only to find the chemical structure was similar to the chemical structure of LSD. Because of his association in high society as a New York banker, Wasson, it is said, was approached by the CIA to find out how the government could use the effects of these mushrooms for mind control experiments. It has been speculated that the CIA funded Wasson and accompanied him on a second trip to Mexico.

In 1957, Wasson wrote an article for Life Magazine describing his psychedelic experiences in this small Mexican town, which opened the flood gates of curiosity to the hipster community in America. People started flooding into this town to find and use these psychedelic mushrooms. The town was soon overwhelmed by foreigners, and the sanctity of the mushroom that the religious people of this town held, was destroyed.

The article in Life Magazine exposed and ruined the ceremonial beauty that the mushroom held for these people. Because of the onslaught of foreigners to their town, Maria Sabina became a pariah to the towns people. The mushroom is an integral part of their religion. The mushroom that was so sacred to these people was no longer the secret of this esoteric community. The integrity of the ceremonial mushroom was now diluted and was now part of the hip culture.

Dr. Carl Ruck was a professor at Boston University. His expertise was in the Greek Classics, and he was the head of the Greek classical studies department at B.U. He became more interested in the interpretation of the theatre of Dionysus and the classical Greek plays. Ruck speculated that certain wines and beers were drunk during these plays and that these elixirs were hallucinogenic, unlike today's understanding of wine and beer.

This didn't sit well with the hierarchy of the university staff, and Ruck was drummed out of his positions at the university. His academic credentials were dismissed by academia. He continued his research on the use of psychoactive substances by the ancients. He became friends with Albert Hofmann and Gordon Wasson due to their common interest in psychedelics, and together they wrote the book "The Road to Eleusis," which describes the mystery held by people who trekked to this city near Athens.

He continued his research on the use of "entheogens," a term he coined, meaning the use of psychoactive substances in religious ceremonies. He has unveiled ancient works of art depicting mushrooms and wheat, where ergot grows, in paintings, carvings and pottery, which could point to their use in religious ceremonies.

Dr. Jerry Brown and his wife, Julie, have traveled extensively and have discovered many forms of art depicting the use of mushrooms and grains. They have documented their travels with photos in their book "The Psychedelic

Gospels," a very interesting read. Many books have been written on the use of psychedelics in religious ceremonies in other cultures. Brian Murareskus's book, "The Immortality Key," gives excellent insight into this subject.

It is almost impossible to discount the use of psychedelics in early religions after using psychedelics and experiencing the spiritual effects they have on people. The popular Timothy Leary, who coined the term "turn on, tune in and drop out," greatly impacted the 1960s and 1970s generation. Although, some say because of that impact, LSD became too popularized, and that's when the U.S. government recognized the "dangers" of it and made it illegal. In the 1950s, the government experimented with LSD and "magic mushrooms" on various people in various ways. It was used on soldiers to see if it could be used as a truth serum. it was used on mental patients to see if it would cure mental illnesses such as schizophrenia. And it was used in other experiments that never resulted in what these experiments were intended for. The effects of these mind-altering drugs can help certain mental maladies, but only if used in small doses and by those who understand their positive effects, not by an unqualified government with no idea of how much a safe dose is or how to walk a person through a psychedelic experience. These psychedelic pioneers, Wasson, Ruck, Hofmann, Leary, and a handful of others, realized that LSD is a life-changing substance and changed their lives, and the lives of many others forever.

After their exposure to psychedelics, they saw the world in such a different way that they left their corporate lives and began a life of mysticism and spirituality. In the 1960s and 1970s LSD flourished. It made its way out of the pharmaceutical laboratories and into the street labs. Along with "magic mushrooms" and other psychedelics, a generation of "peace and love" ensued for millions of people, and an "enlightened" generation was the result of these mind-altering "drugs."

I put the word drugs in quotations because, although LSD originally came from a chemistry lab, it was incorrectly lumped in with drugs such as heroin, cocaine, barbiturates, methamphetamines and other controlled dangerous substances by the government, which allowed them to give it the legal label, "Controlled Dangerous Substance." Control is the key word because it allows the government to control its use and make it illegal unless prescribed by a physician. Unlike cigarettes or alcohol, there are no corporate giants from the LSD industry to donate to politicians, so there was no financial influence to peddle to politicians to investigate the pros and cons of LSD. Hard drugs have always been a problem in society, mainly because they are addicting, and the government had no idea of what they were doing when they included LSD in that category. To the government, "a drug is a drug is a drug."

The effects of LSD could be a dangerous influence on a government by a populous that becomes awakened to the power that government wields, similar to the influence that Jesus had on His followers against the Roman elites when trying to change and liberate people's minds. Protests became increasingly popular by this 1960s/1970s generation, and political corruption and government dishonesty came to light. Laws were changed due to the people's redress of government, and politicians became more accountable to their constituency (The Civil Rights Act and The Environment Protection Act, for example).

Psychedelics had a huge part in this government accountability by wakening this peace and love generation through mind-expanding drugs. Hard drugs are dangerous, although most of us, in the 60s and 70s, tried them anyway, youthful indiscretion. LSD and the like aren't "party drugs" and are not addictive. Psychedelics are in a category by themselves. They are psychoactive.

When you take LSD, you don't dance around like a fool or nod in a stupor. When taking LSD, you see things, externally and internally, that awe you.

For approximately eight to twelve hours, you're mentally in a different place. Your senses are extremely heightened. After you "peak," which means you are at the height of your "experience" that could last two to four hours, you'll slowly come back to a more earthly state of mind, but you are still tripping, which can last for up to a day or two more. You'll gradually wean back to where you were pre-trip. After a few trips, you begin to experience a feeling of total connection with everything and everyone, with nature itself.

The first time you trip, you'll feel an unexplainable elation. Most psychedelic experiences are awesome. Once you've opened that door in your mind, your world will never be the same. You'll find yourself searching for something greater, more gratifying. You'll search for answers to things you've never thought of before. You become curious about everything. This is because new doors have been opened to you for you to explore.

It will eventually lead you to a more spiritual place. Some people who ate LSD had bad experiences, a "bad trip," and ended up in a hospital or doing some "crazy" things like talking nonsense or becoming totally detached from reality. I believe these people were either too mentally fragile in the first place or took an extraordinary amount without precaution.

In the sixteenth century, witches were burned at the stake. These witches, mainly women, were accused of being witches because they were found writhing around on the ground or acting in some insane way as if being possessed by the devil.

In the Field Museum in Chicago, an exhibit tells the story of these so-called witches. The exhibit is of pieces of rye, barley and wheat. It explains how these grains were grown during an extraordinarily rainy season and that these grains spoiled because of the abundance of rain. Ergot grows on wet or moist rye, barley and wheat, and it is now believed that these women ingested these grains and were driven insane by the ergot-infected grains. This is a sad commentary on the supposed era of witchery. But no one knew of ergot and its effect on humans, so these people were killed out of ignorance. It wasn't until 1943 that the connection between ergot and LSD was discovered and its effect on the mind.

In the 1960s and 70s, when you took a hit of "acid," there was no telling what measured amount you were taking. This could account for "bad trips." Like any drug taken in excess, psychedelics could be harmful. Psychedelics bring you to a different reality and mental plane, but you will eventually float back to your pre-psychedelic world as the effects wear off. These bad experiences gave psychedelics a bad name, another reason the government classified LSD as a CDS. Many of my contemporaries, after tripping regularly, dropped out of the "hum-drum" society they were raised in and followed a more spiritual path, as did those chemists years before and maybe as people also did thousands of years ago.

The "bad trips" could have been the inception of Hell thousands of years ago. And Heaven may have come from the spirituality that comes from the mind-expanding beauty of a good trip. "Peyote and magic mushrooms were also considered a CDS". But in the mid-nineteen nineties, the U.S. government legalized it for consumption by certain American Indian tribes and legalized its use for those tribes based on religious freedom, a Constitutional right. For years prior to the discovery of LSD from ergot, people of the "civilized" world had no mystical, spiritual, or psychedelic experiences. Except for the indigenous peoples of Central and South America, American Indians, and some northern Siberian peoples, the civilized world never had their Divine light lit from a psychedelic experience.

The ceremonial consumption of mushrooms and natural plant hallucinogens that aroused spirituality in those cultures was considered absurd by the so-called civilized world. The mescaline and peyote-eating cultures were thought of as unsophisticated. But when LSD and magic mushrooms hit the streets of the "civilized" world, people, mostly the younger generation, realized how the ceremonial use of psychedelics could open their spirit doors as it did for those unsophisticated cultures. A new wave of enlightened culture was about to hit the streets in the early 1960s. Until then, alcohol and cigarettes were the popular drugs. Make way for LSD and pot.

"Turn on, tune in and drop out" was the mantra of the 1960s/70s generation that defied the unenlightened, alcohol-laced society of our parents. We were becoming a new culture, escaping the authority of the unaware "lonely people." Like cultures before us, our "rite of passage," our enlightenment, was from the effects of these psychedelic "drugs," whether we knew it or not at the time. Unless you've experienced a chemically or a natural substance (peyote, ayahuasca, etc.) induced "trip," don't mock or dismiss the effects of psychedelics. There are many ways to spiritual enlightenment, and these substances are certainly one of those ways. Yoga, meditation, extreme solitude, fasting and prayer (Jesus spent forty days in the desert alone) are other ways of reaching a spiritual state of enlightenment. When used in the correct environment and with the correct dosage, psychoactive substances will open doors in your life that are inexplicable, resulting in a spiritual reckoning.

A lot of people of the 1960s and 1970s generation ended up "seeing the light" and just wanted to be left alone from the ever-present bore of the nine to fivers. We started communes, headed for the hills and tried to live off the land without government intervention. There were communes all over the country where people lived off the land, smoked pot and ate psychedelics. After some hard times in these communes, most people left and rented communal houses instead. We realized that living off the land was a hard life. So we pooled our resources and rented houses. Living with essentials like running water and heat in the winter was much more practical and fun.

We did a lot of camping and traveled to huge outdoor concerts. Returning to a place with a roof over our heads and hot running water was more enjoyable. Some people "tripped" once or twice, which was enough for them. Taking the wrong dose or dosing in the wrong environment or with the wrong people could be a frightening experience and discourage some from ever tripping again. On the other hand, some of us continued using and arrived at the "drop out" part of the "turn on, tune in and drop out" mantra and became the "anti-societal misfits" of the time.

As we grew older, some lost that "free bird" state of mind, that "leave me alone" mindset and fell back into society. Some didn't. It became necessary for those who entered into society and started families to make money to support their families and loved ones. We realized that Capitalism wasn't such a bad thing as long as it wasn't abused. Greed can flourish from Capitalism, and that is the problem that governments have. Governments take money, through taxes, that an honest society earns and wastes it on useless, wasteful programs or payback to their political donors.

Those of us who put one foot back into the material world got a job and lived a "normal" life but still had one foot in the world of enlightenment, contentment, peace, love, psychedelia and Godhead. Of course, most of us smoked pot (marijuana), which was also a CDS, but it kept us in a good, anti-establishment mood, and still does. In recent years even pot has become an acceptable part of society. States are legalizing it, slowly but surely, for its "medicinal" value.

Some states have legalized it for recreational use. Hopefully, one day it will be realized that psychedelic substances can also be used to benefit society. Studies have found that micro-dosing, which is taking very small doses of LSD or psilocybin, can help with depression, alcoholism or PTSD. Micro-dosing also enhances one's creative prowess. There are advantages to mild psychedelic experiences, but convincing the government of this will be a steep uphill battle.

The 60s and 70s generations were looked at as utopianists. We did live in a state of mind that we wished everyone would live in. We were labeled "the beautiful people," "flower children," and for a good reason. Through our psychedelic experiences, we thought we could change the world into this beautiful place that we were experiencing.

We were changed. Our minds were liberated from worldly wants and desires. We wanted everyone to live in peace and harmony with ideals that were mostly unattainable, which is what we were mocked for. But we were in a beautiful place in our minds. We were beautiful. We walked with the peaceful, loving

JOHN POWERS

God within us. We were the psychedelic generation. Thank you, Ruck, Hofmann and Wasson and the other psychedelic pioneers.

CHAPTER 3
THE SEARCH

In most religions, the quest is to find peace and happiness through the love of God, a higher spirit, or some higher power. Dedicated souls search their whole lives for this Heaven on Earth, and some eventually find it. The constant search for God is itself a gratifying experience. Staying on a straight and narrow spiritual path is a rewarding but difficult life, and finding God is the ultimate reward. But where is God? In heaven? Where is heaven?

Most religious scholars agree that heaven is

not a place but a reward that the souls of the faithful will attain after death, the afterlife. Teaching that you must live a virtuous life so that when you die, your soul will live on in Heaven, or some form of paradise, is an idea planted in the believer's heads from early in their lives by most religions. This Heavenly paradise is where God exists. The church teaches that God is "out there" and that you will join Him when you die if you live a virtuous life. The question of where God exists is ambiguous. Is God "out there" to be joined after death or here in our hearts and minds, or both?

Most Christians don't question the teachings of the church that God is in Heaven. So is the place to search for God internal, in our hearts and minds, or external, in a church, mosque or synagogue? I see God in everyone, although the God realization is dormant in most people and waiting to be discovered by those people. When you realize the God within is when your spiritual light is lit, and that is when you'll see God in everyone, here and now. This is the ultimate epiphany, and this is when you'll live with love, happiness, contentment, joy and no fear of death. Psychedelics can open doors in the mind allowing the dormant God in you to awaken.

In 1945 the Dead Sea Scrolls were discovered in a place called Nag Hammadi, Egypt, which unveiled more questions about Christianity. Writings by Apostles other than Mathew, Mark, Luke and John were discovered. But their gospels were curiously not included in the Bible. It is speculated that Constantine decided which gospels should and should not be allowed in the Bible at The Council of Nicaea in the early 300s and allowed only the gospels of Mathew, Mark, Luke and John to be in the Bible. This scenario is denied by most Christian scholars.

Most believe these four Gospels were the truest stories of Christ's life and were the most accepted documentation of Jesus. These four Gospels were supposedly written and accepted by the Christian ministry in the second century A.D. which negates the idea that Constantine chose the four Gospels in the New Testaments. The gospels of Phillip, Andrew, Judas, Peter, Thomas, Mary Magdalen and others were among the gospels discovered at Nag Hammadi that are not in the Bible. Why weren't their gospels included in the Bible? These people were as close to Jesus as Mathew, Mark, Luke and John. Did these other Apostles have something to say that the church hierarchy didn't want to be heard?

The Gnostics believed so. The Gnostics, from the Greek word "gnosis," meaning "knowing" or "to know," have a slightly different outlook on Christianity and Jesus . As opposed to Orthodox Catholics, Gnostic Christians believed more in the spirit of Jesus message, the "word" that Jesus preached and that the Holy Spirit is in all of us. They believed that there is a Divine spark in all of us, waiting to be lit and that the path to the Almighty is to be found by searching inward, which is the same as meditation in Eastern religions. In the two thousand years since Jesus, I believe the original Christian way has gotten as convoluted as the game we played as kids called telephone . If there are ten people in a row and the first person tells the person next to him or her a phrase, by the time that phrase is told to the tenth person, it is totally jumbled and is nothing like the original phrase.

I believe this is what happened to the original idea of Christ's "word." The Bible was re-written many times over and interpreted in multiple languages. Words of one language can mean something different in another language. For example, the words "nowhere" and "now here" are spelled exactly the same. It is how they are translated that determines their meaning. Is God nowhere or now here? By the time the Bible was interpreted many times over in many different languages, its meaning had to have been convoluted. Jesus told the people of his time to find God within, to look inside yourself and to find that peace and happiness within, which is where God resides and that God is in you as it is in Him. Heresy, maybe, but many religions meditate to find this inner Nirvana. Buddhism, Hinduism, American Indians, Mexican Indians, and many other religions and cultures all seek God by looking inward. Taking certain substances could also open your spiritual eyes no matter what your religion is, if any at all, and many cultures use mind-altering substances to do so.

Prayer is comforting, but to whom are we asking when we pray for something? People pray to God in heaven or certain saints or religious figures who reside there. Remember, heaven is not a place but a state of mind. So, how do we get to that state of mind, "mind" being the telling word? We talk through our God within, which is the way, I believe, prayer was intended. People pray to God above, but where is above? That depends on where on earth you are standing. Or is above anywhere other than inside the heart and mind? And is God male or female? Maybe there is no above or below. Maybe the individual who finds God within can eliminate these earthly questions by looking inward with prayer or meditation. God is a spirit that has no gender or race.

Whether Christian, Jew, Buddhist, Muslim, Hindu or any other organized faith, even Atheism, we all have the ability to find our God within if we believe in the first place that there is a "higher power." Within is where to start the search, and within is where you may find that "Higher Power." By "Higher Power," I mean the power of being able to live content with peace and love as your guiding principles.

Open your eyes to the world around you and see that mayhem, hate, destruction and ignorance are everywhere. But close your eyes and go to that place inside your mind where all that tumult can be left behind, even if just for a moment in time. With practice that is where, in solitude, you will find peace, contentment, love, Heaven or whatever you wish to call "It." It is a totally peaceful, serene place where no one else is. Whatever you call "it," it's your own

Heaven, your own way, your own church, your own path to your own God. The mind is where "it" emanates from, and the mind can be affected by prayer, meditation, solitude, fasting or psychoactive substances.

The dedication by the clergy of some religions is amazing. Hours of prayer or meditation every day are the main parts of their search for God. But not only by clergy. Some believers go to church every day and serve the church in one way or another. This loyalty gives a rewarding sense of closeness to God, which is very admirable. But there are some religions that don't require a church. The body is the church in many Eastern religions. Meditation multiple times a day will bring you close to your God in Hinduism and Buddhism. Kneeling and facing toward Mecca in prayer five times a day, for Muslims, brings them close to their God, whether inside or outside of a mosque. The point is that there is no specific place to find God other than inside your mind, which is where all prayer and meditation begin. With psychedelics, the path to whomever your Almighty is wide and clear, and all you have to do is walk down that path.

CHAPTER 4
A NEW GUY IN TOWN

Throughout time there have been many cultures that have had many Gods. The God of Air, the God of Water, the God of Earth, Love, Hate, Wind, Fire, you name it, there was a God for it. Ancient cultures understood the value of nature's wonders and assigned Gods to them. In the earliest times, different cultures understood that the earth produced food, the rain and sun fed the earth, and the wind spread the seed. They learned that lightning could start fires that could destroy their crops and homes. They learned that there were seasons, floods, and droughts and that the earth could help heal people by using certain plants.

The use of plants was the earliest form of pharmacology. There were no laboratory-produced chemicals to heal wounds or stop disease. There were only naturally grown remedies, and the more these remedies were explored, the more different effects to the body and mind were discovered. From healing and soothing aloes to mind altering mushrooms, these naturally grown substances were exploited for medicinal and ceremonial purposes. If you got a cut or a rash, you could be healed by spreading some plant based serum on it. If you want to see God, eat a few mushrooms.

The Jewish religion believes that a Messiah will eventually come along and save them, the "chosen people". So when Jesus came along preaching His messianic "word", He was shunned by most Jews and Pagans of that time. This new "word" that Jesus preached disturbed many people but woke up a lot more. Here comes this guy professing that He was sent by "God the Father" to enlighten the world. In a few short years, people spread the word about this man who had a lot to say about living by a code of morals and believing that there is a more sanctified life of peace and love to live by.

The Roman government realized they had to shut Him up before too many people began believing and following His preaching. Far out that this man thought He had all the answers to life and that He was the Messiah sent from God that the world was waiting for. What He was saying, the "word", had people realizing that the individual, not the government, has the power in their lives to obtain peace and love if they searched for the God within. And that this God within is more powerful than any government.

The "word" spread like wildfire. Believe in love and peace, treat people the way you would like to be treated, humility, tolerance, forgiveness, and sacrifice are things that will get you closer to a more glorious life, namely living in parallel with God. This was His message. This was what He preached. Walk a mile in His shoes, so to speak, and your life would be more fulfilling. This was blasphemy to the elites. But the more this belief spread, the more the believer's lives were in danger and, consequently, the more the Roman government had to stop him, and they did. But it was too late, and all the followers at that time started believing and living a more spiritual way of life that still exists today by following His message.

Christianity was becoming bigger than the government. But what was lost in this new movement was how these followers got on this spiritual path. Did mind altering substances have anything to do with it? Were His words alone enough to open their minds to this way of life? Was Jesus so unique that He was born enlightened? Or did He have a little help from his friends, like those who traveled to Eleusis? Were psychedelic substances involved? Were the miracles and visions in the Bible actually miracles, or were they hallucinations from "breaking bread" and drinking ceremonial wine with other believers? When looking at these "miracles" and "visions" from a psychedelic point of view, they make a lot more sense.

Auras painted around holy peoples' heads in artwork from those days are similar to the auras one sees around people when in a psychedelic state. Auras are a hallucinogenic effect of psychoactive substances. Where did these auras in paintings and in other depictions of these saintly people come from, if not from the effects of hallucinogens?

Turning water into wine is as simple as putting a magic mushroom solution, or an ergot solution, into the water, which would cause visions and hallucinations. Wines and beers were not the same then as wines and beers of today. Fifteen hundred years before Christ, in Eleusis, people experienced some kind of life changing spiritual event after drinking a concoction called kykeon. It hasn't been proven yet, but it is believed that this was a psychedelic concoction. In the nineteen sixties and seventies, we dosed people the same way. If you were with a group of people at a party or at some "hippie" house, you had to watch what you got offered to eat or drink.

Brownies laced with pot or any drink laced with LSD were commonplace. A lot of dosing went on in the 1960s and 70s. Remembering that nobody really knows exactly what beers and wines were made of in those days thousands of years ago, we do know that wheat and barley and rye were used and that ergot grew on these grains. There was plenty of psychoactive stuff around to brew up and ergot, the base ingredient of LSD, and the mold that grows on wheat, barley and rye, is an ingredient in the making of beer and bread. The wine fermentation process was also very crude. There were no sulfites or sulfates or preservatives, only fermented grapes and who knows what else was included in the wine making process. These beliefs and opinions are not only my own. People who have had mind altering experiences understand the possibility that the use of psychedelics in ancient times is very probable.

There are many natural hallucinogens on this planet, and back in those times, people could have been under the influence of these substances, unintentionally or intentionally, and had seen and done things that today are interpreted as miracles and or visions. If you have ever read "Revelations" in the Bible, you might agree that John, the author, was influenced by some kind of substance.

A lot of visions were seen by people back then. There were no processed foods in ancient times. Everything eaten, except meats, was grown. Herbs and spices were picked from the fields. No one knows exactly what ingredients went into their meals, but it's not a stretch to believe some psychoactive stuff was thrown into the pot.

They didn't have the luxury of going to a store to buy processed food. Everything eaten and drunk was naturally grown. It is inevitable that something psychedelic was picked in the fields and ingested at mealtime or when they wanted to commune with God. These people had to have been under some kind of external influence. It's hard to imagine that they woke up every day and lived in a world of seven headed dragons and seeing figures with human heads on animals and animal heads on humans, as revealed in Revelations, without being under some kind of psychedelic intoxicant. Why don't we see angels or devils or have some of the visions today that the people of Biblical times saw? From personal experience, I have had some strange visions while tripping on LSD.

In the Catholic religion, the guilt of sin is emphasized early in one's life. The Catholic religion teaches that if you have sins on your soul when you die, you'll go straight to Hell. Or, live a good clean virtuous, sinless life, and you will go to Heaven when you die. I believe that Heaven and Hell are to be found within one's "self". That there is life after death is impossible to know. It may be that if people never find the goodness within themselves in this life, they will live their life in what is believed to be Hell. And conversely, if one finds peace and happiness, love and joy, in this life, they will have found what is believed to be Heaven.

The only afterlife, I believe, is the memory of a person by the living that keeps that person alive in our hearts and minds. The bigger the impact a person makes on their friends and family while alive will determine how long that person's memory will stay with us. Jesus impact was eternal, as was Buddha, Shiva, Mohammad and other spiritual leaders. There may be a continuum of life or consciousness when we die. Image life as a train with no beginning and no end that we get on, called birth, and get off after a time, called death. The train's life is forever, our life is temporary and that our soul or consciousness stays on that train after our body gets off. I may be totally wrong when it comes to the afterlife. Our souls might stay on the train after we die and exists in an afterlife after the body departs the train.

It would be wonderful to live eternally in some mystical paradise. The faithful try to earn entrance to that place, Heaven, by living a virtuous life in the here and now. The afterlife is a comforting goal to aim for. The reuniting with passed family, friends and God is the ultimate reward if there is life after death, but no one knows what happens when we die, so live a good life here and now in case there is no afterlife, and you will be remembered by your friends and family in a positive light.

Some people live their lives in hellish situations and are the kindest people you will ever know. Some people live a life of decadence, greed and extravagance and are the meanest, worse people you will ever know. Does the kind person live in Heaven or Hell? Does the mean person live in Heaven or Hell? The kind person will find their Heaven through faith beyond the material world, even if tortured physically or mentally as Jesus was. The mean person may never experience the rewards of heaven on earth because of the barrier of unkindness that keeps them from experiencing virtue unless they find the light of God within.

There is good and evil in this world, and if one is taught the virtues of life and how to seek out these virtues, they will find that living a morally healthy life is more rewarding and more satisfying than living a life of evil. The path of goodness is the path to God. That path starts and ends by looking inward, which is where I believe, the spiritual prophets told the world to look and that God is in all of us. Was Jesus telling the world that He found God within and that everyone can find this common God within? Was He saying we can find what He found through prayer or meditation or something that will open your mind to peace and love, which includes psychedelics? And that you'll find that heavenly paradise that you seek within. You don't have to look any farther than in your heart and mind to find Heaven. As the famous book by Baba Ram Das says, "Be, Here, Now".

As we get older and wiser, we look at life more seriously. Most elders gain wisdom from the perspective of time on earth. Elders tend to eventually "see the light" through what they have learned and experienced. At some point, we face the inevitable that we are mortal. Although some people never see that light, others "get it" at different stages of life.

We realize the importance of doing good, helping others, treating people the way we want to be treated, and when we realize these things, we become happier and more content with our life. There is a rewarding feeling when we help or do for others. There is a satisfaction that comes with age and wisdom. Those who never "get it" end up living in their own personal "hell", dissatisfied with their lives, always angry about something and blaming others for their unhappiness.

Spiritual people, those who have discovered the rewards of living a virtuous life, are most content. Finding that way of life is one of life's mysteries, and following certain pathways to this enlightenment is a way of obtaining this satisfaction of contentment. This is where God is. Finding that calm, peace, love, Utopia, Nirvana, and Heaven is the objective of living a happy life. Even though life throws roadblocks in our way occasionally, some harder to overcome than others, we eventually, in time, overcome those roadblocks. This is where faith for the spiritually minded can help. This is where the question of "How can God do this" is asked. This is where there is no answer for those who believe someone or something, God, is "out there".

Finding peace of mind can only be found within. We may never find the strength to overcome these roadblocks, but if we do find this inner peace, this is where you will find the God within you.

At any point in one's life, a change from an

evil or bad way of life can be made. A person can see the negative errors of their ways and start a new, more positive way of living by shedding the old life and starting anew. This is being "born again" in some Christian circles. It follows the teachings of Jesus. The ancients called this "dying before you die".

In short, it is simply living a new, more spiritual life. When you know you have lived a virtuous life, you will shed your fear of death. Psychedelics bring you to this realization. Could the key to unlocking heaven's door be no farther than within? It is a fact that for thousands of years, people ate and drank things that opened their minds to spirituality. It is undisputed by people who have taken psychedelics and other psychoactive substances that psychedelics will put you on the path to spirituality.

Ergot, psilocybin, ayahuasca, mescaline are all plant-based natural substances that have been used for centuries in spiritual ceremonies by various cultures, and the effects that they have on people are undeniable. Mushrooms are a prime example of an easily gotten food that has been growing on earth forever. There are hundreds of types of mushrooms which have different effects on the mind and body.

It is very possible that these mushrooms had been ingested thousands of years ago, and their effects on people back then opened their minds to spiritual enlightenment. Mushrooms are still used today in certain cultures for spiritual communion with God. Some hieroglyphics of ancient Egypt, drawings by cave dwellers, paintings by ancient Greeks, and carvings on rocks found all over the world indicate this.

There are drawings of people with bird heads, humans with wings and three headed dogs, Medusa with a head full of snakes, and Poseidon with his trident to stir the oceans. These Gods had to have been the result of some fantastic hallucinations. A lot of these paintings and carvings have people holding wheat or some kind of grain, which, when it starts to mold, produces ergot, the base ingredient in LSD.

Mushrooms are seen in many ancient paintings and carvings. People putting things into urns is also seen in ancient paintings. Could they have been dosing wine or water with some kind of hallucinogen? Does turning water into wine at Cana ring a bell? Was this new guy in town trying to tell us something? Were Jesus teachings the culmination of all prior Gods? Did He try to tell the world to search for that one true God that exists in our hearts and minds?

CHAPTER 5
GODHEAD

T he many religions in the world all profess that their God is the only God. Wars have been fought over whose belief is the true pathway to the Almighty. Jesus, Mohammed, Yahweh, Buddha, and Vishnu are all different prophets who lead you to God. I believe that there are as many pathways to God as there are individuals that all lead to the same place. Let me clarify. When we seek God through prayer, or meditation, or faith, or fasting or extreme solitude, we find that connection in our hearts and minds, no matter what religion. Whether in a group of people, in a church, synagogue, mosque, or in a room by yourself, or on a mountain top or in a desert, we talk to God through channels in our mind. We look to open the door in our mind that God lives behind.

Finding and opening that door is when you realize God lives in you, and you can have a personal relationship with God. If everyone on earth found peace and love in their hearts and minds, that would be the heavenly paradise most religions search for. Psychoactives are analogous to the key to that door. Many people never get curious enough to find out what is behind that door and deny that there is a spiritual life to be lived. Psychoactive substances lead you to that door and hand you the key. They will actually open that door and push you through.

There are approximately two and a half billion Christians that all believe Jesus is "the way". There are approximately two billion Muslims that believe Mohammed is "the way", and there are approximately sixteen million

Jews still waiting for their Savior. It's estimated that half a billion people practice Buddhism or study Vedantism. No matter which religion one follows, we all go through our minds to commune with God. Our mind projects what, or who, God is.

Our mind, our consciousness, is what connects us to God. Open the mind, alter the consciousness, and you might find the path to God sooner. When we start praying or meditating or just talking to whomever we believe the Almighty is, chemicals in the brain start synapsing, which allows us to connect with whomever or whatever God we are seeking. When I say "God", the definition of the God of whom I am speaking can have multiple connotations.

There are different interpretations of God for different religions, but the aim is the same in most religions. We seek that place of peace and love and happiness and contentment, which is who and where our personal God resides. The two and a half billion Christians all believe that Jesus is the Savior, saving us from the evils of the world. But each one of those two and a half billion people goes through their individual minds to commune with God.

It's as if two and a half billion people are telephoning the same person but all on their own individual phones. A group of people can gather and pray for something, but each person is praying individually using their own Mind-God connection. Would it not stand to reason that if there was something that could expand your mind, you would get a better, clearer, or new connection? It's similar to expanding your broadband connection for your internet service.

Expanding your mind with psychedelics gives you a clearer connection with God. If you have never taken a psychedelic, you couldn't know that clearer, mind expanded communication with God that I am trying to convey. There are probably less than one percent of God seeking people who have connected with their God through psychedelics, but that connection is strong and true. When you pray or meditate or fast or seclude yourself or take a dose of a psychedelic, you are opening the door to peace, love, happiness, joy, and contentment right here and right now, on earth, and in this life. The belief of most religions is that we will end up in an eternal paradise when we die if we lead a certain religious lifestyle. But maybe Heaven can be found here and now in this life on this planet.

As we go through life, we are confronted with temptation. Defying our parents in our youth, defying authority, and defying the laws of government lead to an immoral life, which leads to different degrees of punishment. Defy your parents as children, and you'll get your cell phone taken away. Defy the government, and you could end up in prison. Lie, cheat, steal, or commit any number of immoral acts and you will live with a guilty conscience that will be a stain on your soul forever, that is, if you have a conscience. There is no guilt without a con-science.

In the Old Testament, the ten commandments are the sins that we should abstain from. Sins in Catholicism must be confessed and be absolved before we die in order to make it into Heaven. Your conscience is what determines what is right or what is wrong. So we have to decide which path we want to follow, a moral or immoral lifestyle. Although most of us live somewhere in between, we tend to lean toward the moral end of the spectrum.

The whole objective of most religions is to point you in a moral direction. In the psychedelic world, this option is clear. You realize the beauty of life, so why ruin it with the burden of immorality. If you decide to resist goodness, you will end up living in your own personal degree of "Hell". Naturally, there are stories of evils committed by people who had taken psychedelics (the Manson family, for instance). But there is more to that evil story than their use of psychedelics. What wasn't disclosed is what other harmful drugs these people were on or what evil was instilled in them previously.

What is fascinating is the decisions we make, guided by our beliefs, which are usually instilled in us from childhood. If we teach our children to have respect for life and to not harm living things, ninety percent of those people grow into morally sound adults. Children with no guidance and no understanding of right and wrong will most likely grow into the destructive part of society. Parents with good morals tend to raise good-moral children.

Fear of wrongdoing or sinning is instilled in the Catholic child. Teaching children to understand right from wrong is more effective than instilling fear in them. Once a person knows what's right and what's wrong, or what's good or what's evil, will help that person make the right decisions in their lives. Most of the time, the righteous path is chosen. Teaching this way of life, and only this, should be the purpose of the church, not instilling fear in children, in my opinion.

Atheists and people who believe that there is no higher power or God are fine with me.

Most Atheists, or Agnostics, do believe that there is right and wrong, good and evil, love and hate in this world. They believe that these are simply earthly emotions and want nothing to do with an inner or outer spirit. Most spiritual people believe that there "is" someone or something that tells them to strive for goodness, righteousness and love and avoid hatred and evil and that this love can be found through prayer or meditation, namely God. This is the decision we make when we get in touch with our conscience. Some believe God is "out there", and some believe God is "within".

Most Orthodox religions are the "out there" believers, whereas Gnostic Christians and some eastern religions believe God is within. This is one reason Gnostics are shunned by the Orthodox Catholic community. Gnostics believe more in the spirit of the Christian "word" rather than the Jesus story of the resurrection. As mentioned earlier, the Dead Sea Scrolls revealed a new insight into

Christianity.

The writings of some Apostles that were found in the Dead Sea Scrolls that weren't allowed in the Bible may have had some different knowledge of the teachings and visions and hallucinations and goings on of those early day Christians. These people could have been heavily influenced by psychoactive eats and drinks. They might have communed with God the way people of all time and many cultures throughout history experienced the "spiritual beyond" with the use of psychoactive plants, including a variety of mushrooms.

The writings of these outcast Apostles may have conflicted with the early church's beliefs. From the beginning of life on earth, through ancient Egypt, through the 1960-70s generation and beyond, people have been freeing their minds and "seeing God" with the use of psychoactive substances. Why not early Christians?

Let me deviate a bit. Belief in extraterrestrials is a popular topic these days, and although there is no actual proof that anyone has ever seen or communicated with one, there is a belief that beings from "outer space" have occupied earth in the past or even presently. It may be true, but when I listen to what is supposed to be proof of these beings, it's hard to reason. The proof is very unreliable. As vast as the universe is, the odds that extraterrestrial beings would land on earth, with all the intelligence it took for them to get here, and would not make contact with us, is incredulous. When I hear or see what people believe is proof of these ancient or current ETs, it makes more sense that people of the past were inebriated on some mind altering substance and were actually hallucinating.

Drawings and carvings on cave walls and on pyramid walls and on cliff dwellings could be their expressions of hallucinations encountered while under the influence of mushrooms,

cannabis, ergot, nightshade, belladonna, ayahuasca, or some other mind altering substance,
of which there were and are, many. I do believe
there have been past civilizations that lived on
Earth thousands or millions or even billions of
years ago. Some of the structures discovered
from the past were built with incredible engineering skills. My opinion is that these structures were from earthly beings, not extraterrestrials. If these earliest civilizations ate certain
plants, cocoa leaves, for instance, which is the
base of cocaine, and elevates your energy level,
combined with other "foods of the Gods", for
instance, psychedelic mushrooms, or other
psychoactive plants, which were undoubtedly
growing thousands of years ago, their creativity
and engineering skills could have been the results of these substances. I may be totally
wrong, and this is just my opinion, but to me,
these are more questions about mind altering
substances that might have been discovered
and used by people thousands of years ago.

There was an expression in the 1960s that

summed up how we felt when high on LSD, and that expression was "far out". I believe these ancient people were "far out" the same way the trippers of the 1960s-70s generation were. Until there is actual communication between E.T.s and earthlings, I will remain a skeptic.

CHAPTER 6
FREEDOM

Governments, dictatorships, monarchies, and all the elite ruling classes, have always been confronted with opposition from the "working class", the proletariat. It is innate in people to resist being told or ordered what to do from an elite, authoritative ruling class. Freedom is most sacred, and to have freedom taken away or stifled by these elites, which is what governments do to control their populations, will stir defiance in most people or groups of people. Freedom does not come from governments, but it can be taken away by governments.

Our freedom is supposed to be protected by the government. Freedom is congenital, and as the framers of the U.S. Constitution wrote, freedom is an inalienable right. We are all born free, even if you are born in a country where freedom is not practiced or allowed. It is the controlling government that stifles God-given freedoms. Freedom to speak, to express oneself, to gather, to defend oneself or to practice a religion are freedoms we are born with. Most people, who are born and raised in a freedom loving country, take these freedoms for granted and don't realize the value of freedom until it is taken away.

The United States is a country where freedom is the most valuable right. The governing documents of America make this clear. When one's mind is opened to the fact that freedom is as innate as the God within, one realizes how unimaginable it would be for a ruling class to take one's freedom away. It is sometimes not realized that, incrementally, our freedoms are slowly chipped away at. When used responsibly, psychoactive drugs amplify how valuable freedom is. One of the major effects of using psychoactive substances is the freedom you realize when you enter the spiritual realm of your consciousness.

In the 1960s and 1970s, the chant of "free your mind" was associated with tripping on LSD or mushrooms. The revelation that people should be free to do what they want to do, without the government interfering and without harming others, became an important part of the 60s and 70s cultural revolution.

A lot of protesting happened back then, mostly because of the Vietnam war and mostly by the generation of peace and love, who were tripping on acid (LSD). Freedom, especially from the grip of government, became another reason for the protest. There is something about psychoactive stuff that opens your mind to questions about why and how it is possible for anyone, or any government, to take our natural-born freedoms away. The right of "freedom to assemble" and "freedom of expression" by protest was met with violence by the U.S. government in the 1960s and 70s. People died for simply expressing themselves (the Kent State deaths).

The inalienable right of people to gather and express themselves, being met with violence, was inexcusable. In the 1930s, 40s and 50s, people were hosed, whipped, beaten and killed for expressing their desire to be free and equal amongst men. In some countries, North Korea, for example, the word freedom isn't even in their vocabulary.

In countries like North Korea and some Mid-Eastern countries, there are no freedoms, even though you are born with the absolute God given right to be free. In some Mid-Eastern countries, women are treated as slaves. They must walk behind their husbands when allowed out in public, and they must be totally covered except for their eyes and can only speak when spoken to. Keeping people under-fed is a tactic of some dictatorships. A mal-nourished citizenry will do almost anything for scraps of food, including succumbing to the government dictates. Starvation equals control which is the main source of power for evil dic-tatorships.

Some folks believe that human rights aren't given by a higher power, but ironically, that freedom of expression is their right. No matter where you believe freedom comes from, you are born with the right to speak, think, express, defend yourself, believe in God and live peace-fully. Prayer is not allowed in countries like North Korea, only allegiance to the "Supreme Leader". These people that live in fear of their government revere only their supreme leader, their President. They are raised in fear and would not dare search, through prayer, to find the God inside them. This is the sad result of the absents of freedom. Be thankful if you were born in America or another freedom loving country, and have the right to believe in a God if you so choose.

After using psychoactive substances and realizing the God within, you'll find a oneness with everything. Through the psychedelic experience, you'll realize that we are all connected in a universal, cosmic way.

Whether you call it nature or God or nirvana or moksha or whatever you label "it", you will feel connected to "it". You will have opened the door to "spiritual enlightenment". You will have a new outlook on life, and you will know yourself and your spiritual path better than ever before. When you have awakened this awareness in you through the psychedelic experience, a certain confidence and curiosity take hold of you. You become more aware of societal wrongs. You realize the freedoms that all people should enjoy. You realize the beauty of the world we live in. And you become an opponent of the suppression of freedom.

What is frustrating is the grip that the elitists have on the "useful idiots", the uninformed that just "go along with the program", and "programmed" they are. This is the part of society that does whatever their government tells them without question. These are people who don't question government dictates and put too much faith in what politicians promise. This is very frustrating to those who feel they have "seen the light" and believe in our individual freedom.

Most people try to live an ethical and productive life and take advantage of the freedoms they are endowed with. It is an eternal battle to hold on to our natural born freedoms. Governments from the beginning of organized governments, have been trying to restrict the freedoms of their populous in order to control them. This is the intoxication of power that politicians try to hold on to. Freedom, even though innate, ironically comes with a cost. Freedom is not free. When government control becomes overwhelming and tries to restrict our freedoms, we must fight back peacefully and, hopefully, without conflict. The freedom to choose a lifestyle where one can choose what is good for the individual without being told what we can eat, drink, smoke or do in a responsible and peaceful way is a goal we must all strive for to make the world a better and freer place.

Unfortunately, the governing elites who wield the power to make laws that restrict our right to live free become blind with that power, and that is where resistance from the populous begins. Throughout the ages, governments have tried to control the populous, and in countries where freedom is suppressed, the government wins.

The Constitution of the United States enumerates and restricts the power of the government of America. The Bill of Rights enumerates the rights of the governed. The psychedelic generation of the 1960s and 1970s enlightened the world to resisting government control and LSD and other psychedelics played a huge part in that fight. The mind freeing effect of psychedelics was the "cat that was let out of the bag". They were the impetus that led to the pushback against a freedom-stifling government and made people more aware of the power that "We The People" had over its government. Thank you, Albert Hofmann and his contemporaries.

CHAPTER 7
THE "WOW" FACTOR

Opening your mind by using psychedelics the first few times will introduce you to a world of wonder and curiosity. It is the ultimate "WOW" factor. I was twenty-one years old the first time I tripped, and as wild a ride as it was, I did not experience anything spiritual at first. I was too naive, too young to know what to expect.

The hallucinations and the psychedelic experience itself was fascinating. I continued tripping for some time afterward. As my trips piled up, I became more serious about life as I became aware of the spiritual world unfolding in me. I was becoming more aware of this new reality I was experiencing. One of the battles one experiences when taking psychedelics is the battle with one's ego.

The ego, or "self", that you were pre psychedelics, fights to hold on to that "self". Psychedelics break you free from that "self," and you can either fight it or go with it. Once you've convinced your "self" to go where the drug takes you, you will feel freer than ever before. You will know your "self" better than ever before. You will see your "self" from a different point of view. You will actually see your pre-psychedelic "self" as opposed to your post-psychedelic "self".

Entering into this new consciousness can be scary to the point of paranoia. It is the release from the ego which you've been comfortable with your whole life, and seeing yourself as a new person with different values that can be frightening. This could be scary at first, but when you see the beauty of what this new reality has to offer, the paranoia diminishes. If and when you stop taking psychedelics, your "Doors of Perception" (Aldous Huxley) to this new outlook on life will never close, they remain wide open. You will have entered through the door of enlightenment, distant from routine society.

When you stop taking psychedelics, you'll drift back into mainstream society. You may do your societal duties, like getting married, having children, working and all the things a "normal" person is supposed to do to fit into society. But your spiritual lamp has been lit, and it will never go out. Your mind will have been freed, and you will forever see life through post-psychedelic eyes.

Because of my Catholic upbringing, after my psychedelic experiences, I became more spiritually curious and started questioning the Catholic religion that I was raised in. Psychedelics opened my God world, and that is when I questioned why I had to go to church to be spiritually connected to the Almighty.

I questioned if I had to be a good Catholic in order to be a good Christian. And do I have to be a good Christian to be a good person? I have two sisters and a brother. We were raised in an Italian/Irish household. My mother went to church almost every day until her passing at age ninety seven. My father passed when I was three years old, so I never got to know him, although I know he was a devout Catholic, according to my mother. My two sisters still go to church almost every day. I went to church every Sunday, as an obedient Catholic, from as early as I can remember until my skepticism in my early twenties.

Catholicism was ingrained in my brain. I never questioned the religious beliefs that were taught to me. But after my psychedelic experiences opened my spiritual door, the questions about the ritual, the rules, the guilt, and the structure of the church all added up to what seemed to me to be a cult-like organization. The confines of the church were stripped away by my psychedelic experience. I reiterate, I am not disparaging the church, I am questioning it from a different point of view. People who have faith in the church, like my sisters, are happy and satisfied with their faith in the church, but I do believe there is a certain amount of blind faith with some of the Christian community. Following what our elders tell us, without question, from generation to generation, is not believing in your religion, it is the definition of blind faith.

The mind-opening experiences of LSD and peyote buttons let me see religion in a different way than my family, and others see religion. I do believe Jesus walked the earth and had a message for the world, which is simple and direct, but I don't believe I have to sit, kneel and stand for an hour in a church in order to adhere to that message. The evolution of the church throughout the centuries, I believe, has become bigger than the original intent of Jesus message.

The ruler Constantine in 320AD, organized and set the rules and regulations for

Christianity and declared Christianity the official religion of the Roman Empire. I believe the Christian doctrine, the "word" that Jesus preached, has been muddled by the church of today due to the contortions the church has gone through for over two thousand years, which resulted in the ritual doctrine one must follow. Constantine's rules for the church severely punished people who didn't obey these rules. The church became tyrannical, hence the crusades eight hundred years later. You either believed and submitted to the church's rules or die.

The church's base message is the Bible. But the Bible can be ambiguously interpreted. It has been rewritten a number of times in a number of languages. If you compare the Jesus doctrine, the "word", to the church doctrine, as two separate entities, you may realize that one is a way of life (the "word"), and the other is more politically structured, having rules, regulations, hierarchy and punishment if you don't abide by its doctrine. I believe that living the way of life that Christ's message was originally intended is simpler than the church's doctrine of today.

There are many Christian churches, Catholic, Protestant, Lutheran, Baptist, and many others, that all believe Jesus Christ is the "Savior". But they each have a different twist on their belief of whose church is the correct way to practice Christianity. On the other hand, there is only one "word", and that "word" is monistic, simple and uncomplicated and can be found within you. Where did this monistic doctrine come from? What mind realized this simple way of life, and when and how did He become aware of this way of life? Could He have had external influences? Was He taught by His elders, or was He enlightened, like so many others before and after Him, by psychoactive substances that were readily available in those days? It isn't known for sure about the first thirty years of Jesus life. He may have been experiencing other philosophies, such as Hinduism or Buddhism or He may have been experiencing psychedelics that heightened His belief of who and where God is.

Christians believe God sent Jesus to save our souls. Why didn't those before Him realize this moralistic way of life and preach what He preached? Saying or doing anything against the existing government or ruling class of the Roman Empire in Jesus time got you tortured and killed. These elitists ruled with fear. They may have been aware of the effects of psychedelics and suppressed their use as governments today suppress the use of some drugs. Maybe Jesus had the courage to stand up for what he believed in and risked that belief of a moral lifestyle by defying this massive, cruel government. Was his mind freed by something that He ate or drank? Was there something in the wine that opened His mind? Did He eat or drink some psychedelic concoction? Did the ergot in the moldy bread have an effect on His and others' minds? Did He realize that the individual who listens to one's inner self, and finds God within, is more personally powerful than any earthly government?

Did He experience the "WOW" factor? In the end, he was tortured and killed for speaking His mind and preaching morality to the masses, in spite of the power of the Roman Empire, in a way that left an indelible way of life on humanity. But not before He stood up to those tyrants and defied their power. He saw the light within. He realized the sanctity of life. He cherished the value of every person and told everyone to trust that "Divine light", that God within. He opened the eyes and minds of the people of His time and for people thereafter. The beauty of the realization of individual freedom is inexplicable, and that is one of the effects of the enlightening psychedelic experience. It is also the result of the psychedelic eating, peace and love generation of the 1960s and 70s movement. Although believers in this new doctrine tried to be clandestine for fear of the heavy hand of the government of the Roman Empire, they spread the word anyway. The word spread and the people rejoiced in this newfound spiritual freedom. Flash ahead two thousand years and compare it to the protests of the "flower children" of the 1960s and 70s who found enlightened freedom through psychoactive substances. The comparison is strikingly similar. Protest the authority of an out-of-control, heavy-handed government, organize those who believe in the freedoms that you believe in, and march in defiance of unjust laws, and you will be figuratively crucified.

CHAPTER 8
BRAIN POWER

I believe that Jesus, Buddha, Vishnu, Mohammed, Mexican Indians, American Indians, shamans and clergy of all the other spiritual cultures communed with their Almighty by affecting something in their brain, which is where all the senses are interpreted. When the brain is activated by a life-threatening experience, a trauma, or a psychoactive substance, it "opens doors" that make one see things differently than they had before that experience. If you have ever survived a near-death experience, your outlook on life was probably changed forever. A heart attack, cancer, stroke or any physical trauma will shake and change your outlook on life.

There is no doubt that once one eats psychoactive stuff, it will also change one's life forever, and you will attain some kind of spiritual awakening and curiosity. After the initial shock from these experiences, it takes time, for most people, for the shock of that experience to quell. The memory of the experience, most likely, becomes indelible, and you will be changed for a long time, probably for the rest of your life. A similar thing happens when you take psychedelics. Your brain reacts, and you enter into a place that you will never forget. We learn from every experience we have in our lives. Experiences are what format our lives. These different experiences help formulate different opinions and views in people, and the psychedelic experience will change your perspective on everything.

Everything we put in our bodies has some kind of effect on us. Eat or drink something with caffeine in it, and your body reacts. Eat or drink something spoiled and your body reacts.

Drink alcohol and your body and mind react. Eat whatever kind of drug, legal or illegal, and your mind and body reacts. Eat LSD or psilocybin or ayahuasca, or any of a variety of psychedelic mushrooms and your mind and body will react, especially your mind. Smoke pot or DMT and the body and mind react. Most people who have taken any psychoactive substances will tell you how these "drugs" opened up new insights into their lives.

In the 1960s and 1970s, a lot of my contemporaries were dosing with psychedelics regularly. There were a lot of guys who thought they were Jesus after a number of acid trips. "Jesus Freaks" were people who had their spiritual light lit to the extent that thrust them onto a spiritual plane that can only be described as feeling what they thought Jesus felt and thought. People who ate psychedelics were enlightened to Christianity, Hinduism, Buddhism and other spiritual philosophies. It is an amazing phenomenon how after ingesting natural psychedelic substances that grow organically, or pharmaceutical mind benders produced in a lab, can change a person's perspective of the world forever.

Ninety-five percent, plus or minus, of people who have tripped on one or more of these substances step over a threshold into a spiritual realm. When you ask people who have had a psychedelic experience about their experience, they will tell you of how they were transformed into seeing the world differently and mostly more positively. They see life through more spiritual eyes.

If you have ever watched a person who is tripping progress through their experience, they'll tell you how beautiful they feel and how removed from their known reality they are. This is because their minds have been "expanded" and are experiencing a new reality, a more "connected to everything and everyone" reality, a different perception of life. You can replace the word "reality" with "world" or "consciousness," but whatever term you use, it is a beautiful, mind-opening experience for most.

Reflecting back on the psychedelic experience, most people will recognize the spirituality of the experience. This common factor of being in a spiritual place is where you'll eventually find your God. First-time trippers may get a bit paranoid because it is such a new and strange experience, which is why it's a good idea to have someone who has tripped before nearby for reassurance. Some people are mentally or emotionally fragile and should stay away from anything mind-altering. Because it is such a new experience, most people feel an indescribable elation and laugh uncontrollably in the first couple hours of their trip, of which there is no marked time. It is a timeless adventure.

When the hallucinations start, this newfound wonderment of colors, moving shapes and forms, and sounds is fantastic. After approximately four to six hours of this new reality, you'll gradually come back "down" to a more controlled awareness, but you are still tripping, although not as intensely. In total, an

LSD trip is about a ten to fourteen-hour excursion. You will still feel the affects of your trip for another day or two, but much milder.

When you reflect back on this "mind-blowing" experience, you will either tell yourself, "Never again" or "Give me another dose". You'll know what to expect the second and third times you trip. But each trip is different because new doors open each time. With each trip things become more serious because you'll see life through more inquisitive eyes. You will, eventually, reach a spiritual zone. Some folks get to this spiritual zone after a dose or two. Some will get there after three or four trips, but psychedelics will inevitably open up your "God door" eventually.

I am not promoting psychedelics, although I feel they can positively affect society. My main interest is the connection between religion and mind-altering pathways to spirituality with psychedelics, of which I believe there is a strong connection.

When I hear preachers talk about how God is going to do this or that, or God said this or that, or how God made it rain, or how God could kill people by causing earthquakes or hurricanes or tornados or other natural disasters, they speak as if God is a flesh and blood person that they can rely on to physically do something about these occurrences. I can understand having faith in a spiritual being, but relying on that spiritual being, or God, to stop or cause natural disasters, is altruistic. These are the people who believe God is somewhere "out there".

If you are praying to someone or something "out there" to fix things, which is what faith is to a lot of people, I don't believe anyone or anything is "out there" to help, although many people do. A lot of people believe in the power of prayer. I believe praying is a "self-consoling" practice that can help you confront your God within. It is a hope or wish that something will or will not happen or change. I believe that praying, like meditating, was originally intended to find comfort within and to connect with the God within, asking the collective God in all of us for peace and tranquility. God, to me, is a reflection of humanity, and if everyone lit their "Divine spark" within, goodness instead of evil would reign, and the "Divine spark" would turn into an inferno of love.

If all of humanity believed in God inside all of us, through a common spirituality, there would be no problems on Earth. If everyone had a common focus on one universal belief of peace and love, there would be no disagreement, no wars, no hate, and no problems. This Utopian dream will never happen, although it is worth striving for. Teaching this concept is the focus of most peace loving religions. But even in peaceful religions, there are discrepancies that foster disagreement. This, along with cultures that profess violence in the name of religion, is why universal Utopia will never exist.

There will always be disagreement amongst

people, religions, cultures, even though most people want to exist peacefully with one and another. Peace and love can only happen individually by searching within yourself; psychedelics can lead you to that peaceful self. You can have peace of mind within, even if no one else around you is at peace with themselves. When you find that peaceful, loving place, you will have found God. The 1960s and 70s generation was enlightened to this peace and love through psychedelics. Ninety-five percent of that generation was focused on peace and love. We found our Godhead with psychedelics.

When Jesus said, "I am the way", I believe that the "I" he is referring to is the "I" in everyone and that the God in Jesus is the same God within all of us waiting to be recognized. The "way" is the spiritual way that He preached. Jesus said, "Eat of my flesh and drink of my blood", which in biblical terms means, to most biblical scholars, be like me, live like me, find the God in you that He found in Him. Jesus knew the God within Him, and

His simple message was that we all have the ability to find peace, love, compassion, tolerance, joy, humility, goodness, forgiveness and sacrifice in ourselves, which is God. If we practice these virtues daily and live by the "golden rule" (do unto others as you would have them do unto you), we can attain a more spiritually satisfying connection to the God within and exude God.

The simple message of living a good clean life is an objective of most religions. To spiritually minded people, everything that Jesus preached at the "Sermon on the Mount" is obvious. Those passages are simply common sense ways of treating your fellow man, spoken by a man who wasn't afraid of being punished by the powers that be. In the world of duality, there are only two ways to live, which are good or evil. Aiming toward good is God's direction. Aiming toward evil is the direction of living a hell-bound life of strife, anger, discontentment and turmoil. The psychedelic experience will point you in a direction that searches for truth and goodness through self-awareness. It may be that in Jesus' day, his sermons were profound. He felt free from the fear of government retribution and that his beliefs and convictions were stronger than his fear of government reprisal. I believe we can understand the preaching of a man whose message I agree with without going to a church. I am approaching my beliefs from the experience of two points of view. I was raised in the ways of the Catholic Church, and I have experienced the way that my spiritual lamp was lit through psychedelics. Again, church is a wonderful place in which to put your faith for those who choose. On the other hand, I do not feel the need for a structured organization in order to understand what spirituality is and to understand the meaning of Jesus' "word".

CHAPTER 9
TRY SOME OF THIS

There are certain substances that influence and activate parts of the brain. Aspirin affects receptors in the brain to block pain. Anesthetics are used to dull pain or sedate a person for surgical purposes. Inhaling things, like menthol, will help clear sinus congestion. Smell something delicious, and the brain will make you salivate. Many ingestible substances make the brain react. The brain is where the effects of things that are smelled, tasted, smoked, touched, heard or seen are generated. The mind is what makes the body react to these senses. When psychedelic substances are eaten or smoked, the brain releases neurotransmitters that will stimulate parts of the brain that may have previously been dormant, and new experiences occur. It is not known exactly how much of the brain is used at any given time.

People who question the spiritual effects of psychedelics are people who have never experienced them. I am not endorsing psychedelics, although I believe they have a positive affect. I am trying to convey to those who haven't had the psychedelic experience not to judge until they know what it is they're judging. Like riding a motorcycle, scuba diving, parachuting from a plane, or doing something you have never done before, people are understandably trepidatious. Some people would never eat certain things because it looks disgusting, or they won't do something because the government advised them not to, or because of fear. If abused, like anything, there are downsides to psychedelics. But, when used responsibly, there are positive reactions to psychedelics, just as there are positive reactions to prescription drugs.

Spiritual awakening is one of the positive reactions of psychedelics. In the early psychedelic days of the 1960s and 70s in America, our generation did not use psychedelics responsibly until we realized the power of these psychedelics. It only took a trip or two to realize that we were experimenting with some serious stuff. The eye-opening effects of psychedelics are powerful yet enlightening. They altered the course of a generation that had a lasting effect on society. They emboldened a generation to promote peace and love, similar to what Jesus professed two thousand years ago.

Mycology is the study of fungi. Mushrooms are fungi. There are millions of types of mushrooms. Some mushrooms are lethal when eaten, and some are tasty and have no adverse effects when eaten. But some mushrooms have psychedelic effects when eaten, so it is advisable to know what kind of mushroom you are eating before you eat them. Mycologists have categorized most mushrooms so that you can know which ones are good for you, which ones are bad for you, and which ones will send you on a psychedelic experience you'll never forget. These are nicknamed "magic mushrooms" and have been growing on Earth longer than humanity.

The root system of mushrooms, mycelium, is extraordinary. It is a fine, hair like system that travels underground, searching for the next place to pop up its mushroom head. It is an intelligent communication system with hundreds of thousands of tentacles under one single footprint. Fungi and mushrooms are an extremely important part of the environment. They seek out dead or decaying life and help in the disintegration process, nourishing the Earth. Paul Stamets is an expert on mushrooms. He has written many books and knows almost everything there is to know about good, bad and psychedelic mushrooms, Mycology.

Terrance McKenna, who was an advocate of "magic mushrooms", theorized that the brains of apes were expanded by eating psychedelic mushrooms in a two hundred thousand-year span, a million years ago. The "Stoned Ape" happened upon these magic mushrooms while foraging for food, and the effects that these mushrooms had on these apes helped them evolve by expanding their minds. Creativity, language, organizational skills and intelligence itself were expanded by opening new channels in the brains of those apes. The apes became more communal, more intelligent, more curious, more driven sexually, and more culturally advanced, according to McKenna. It is well known that ape's brains doubled in size in that two hundred thousand year time period of history, and mushrooms might have been the reason why. This is considered a hypothesis by skeptics and may very well be hypothetical. It is also very feasible that ape's minds were expanded and their brains grew when one realizes the effects that psychedelic mushrooms have on humans.

Constant prayer or meditation are methods of connecting to and understanding the spiritual world. Psychedelics, like magic mushrooms and LSD, will also open the pathways to your spiritual and creative worlds in a way that makes you see everything and everyone connected under one big tent in a curious way. That one big tent, that connection to everyone and everything, to me, is the Almighty we search for. It would be Utopian if everyone on Earth was in this "everyone and everything is connected" state of mind. There would be total peace on Earth. The problem is that evil exists on Earth. Peace, love, tolerance and goodness are antithetical to evil. Good against evil is an eternal battle. The 1960s and 1970s generation may have been floating around in a psychedelic haze, but peace and love, the main mantra of that time, was the objective we sought brought on through the psychedelic experience. Thank you, LSD and magic mushrooms.

CHAPTER 10
SOUL FOOD

The soul is everything you are that is not physical. Your being, your essence, you, is what your soul is. Your soul is where you find your moral compass. Your soul is where your conscience resides. You can't physically touch your soul, you can only spiritually be in touch with it. When you question what is right or wrong, your conscience decides. The soul is where your spiritual world is. We all have a soul, whether we want to acknowledge it or not. The soul is where your "Divine spark" is, waiting to be lit. Imagine that the whole universe is one big soul, and each individual soul could connect to it by opening a pathway between the individual soul and the universal, cosmic, mystical soul, analogous to the umbilical connection between mother and child.

When you find the connection between your individual soul and the universal soul, you are on your way to Nirvana, Utopia, Heaven and oneness with all. You must first acknowledge that you have a soul, which is a spiritual reckoning. This is the oneness you'll experience with psychedelics. In Eastern philosophy, the "third eye" is the pathway to the soul. When we see Eastern religious people with a cosmetic dot on their forehead, that is the point of concentration when meditating, to open the third eye. It is where one focuses to open the spiritual world. It has been discovered that the pineal gland, which is located in the center of the brain, controls our dream state, our circadian rhythm, our creativity and our spiritual world.

The pineal gland reacts to light and dark cycles and releases melatonin, which controls our circadian rhythm. The dream state of mind is also part of the subconscious mind. When meditating, the pineal gland is activated, opening our third eye and allowing us to enter our spiritual consciousness. Concentrating on the center of your forehead with your eyes closed, and using certain breathing techniques, can open the third eye. Psychoactive drugs have an effect on the pineal gland, and this is another way your spiritual door can be opened. The pineal gland is named for its likeness to a pinecone. The pinecone is often seen in ancient carvings and paintings. Pharaohs holding staffs with pinecone heads are depicted in many ancient artifacts and hieroglyphics. Throughout time the pinecone is seen in many works of religious and spiritual art.

One of the staffs that the pope uses has a pinecone head on it, and there is a giant pinecone statue in Vatican square, although I don't think the pope makes the connection between the pinecone and the pineal gland. It may be a coincidence that pinecones are seen throughout the ages in artwork and statues and hieroglyphics, or it may be that the ancients knew the effects that certain substances had on the pineal gland, especially psychoactive substances, of which there were many, then and now. LSD effects the serotonin receptors in the brain, but it's not exactly clear how LSD effects the serotonin receptors, only that it does something to aid in the psychedelic experience. Meditate to open your spiritual door or feed the pineal gland with psychoactive substances, and you'll open the door to your soul.

In Eastern religions, a healthy body and a clear mind are essential to living a spiritual life. In eastern religions, seven energy zones in the body, called chakras, must be kept healthy to keep a healthy body and mind. Some philosophies believe there are up to thirteen chakras, but most rely on the seven chakra theory. These seven energy zones are located up the spine to the crown of the head. The sixth chakra is the "third eye" and is where, when meditating, you will enter your spiritual world. A healthy body helps keep the mind healthy, and a healthy mind makes it easier to connect to the spiritual world, which is where God is.

Many of the world's population goes about their day without a single thought of the spiritual world within them. The gravity of anger, discontentment, anxiety, stress, aggravation and all the negative emotions people experience in their lives keep people from enjoying their spiritual world. The psychedelic experience awakens your spiritual world and puts you in touch with your soul. Psychedelics aren't necessary to open one's door to spiritual enlightenment, but they do offer the switch to turn on the light within.

In recent years experiments with psychedelics have been found helpful in treating people with certain mental illnesses and disorders. The aftereffects of most of those treated found a spiritual awakening. In the 1960s and 70s, we ate psychedelics, not knowing, initially, a big part of our generation would be enlightened to a mystical, spiritual world. We ate psychedelics because it was the thing to do. As more people turned on to psychedelics, we became more aware of the spirit within, and many turned to seek that "higher" realm of the spirit world.

We didn't realize our spiritual awakening at first, but that spiritual awareness eventually shone through, and I, for one, am grateful for that mind-expanding time in my life.

The soul is the connection between the material and the spiritual world. To connect with the soul is the challenge; keeping the soul clean and free of evil is what most religions profess. Our soul stays clean when we live a good, virtuous, wholesome life. Eastern religions believe we are reincarnated, meaning our soul or consciousness will live again after death in the next life in another body. The quality of that next life is determined by how we lived in our previous life. This is called Karma. Eastern religions rely on good Karma to attain Moksha, which is the final freedom from continuous rebirth, or reincarnation, back into the material world. Moksha is the final release from worldly, material desire, which is the ultimate paradise in Eastern religions.

Christians rely on a clean soul to enter the gates of Heaven after death. That we go to paradise after death is a goal worth believing in. But no one knows what happens after death, and if there is no afterlife, all the goodwill we accumulated on Earth to gain entry into this paradise will result in being known as a good person and living with contentment and peace of mind in the here and now. I believe Heaven can be attained here and now. Live a good clean life, and you'll live a more rewarding life on Earth, here and now. The rewards of helping your fellow humans will result in tangible, earthly goodwill. And if there is an afterlife, a heavenly paradise, your cache of goodwill will be applied to your entry into this heavenly paradise.

Prayer or meditation are ways to get in touch with your soul and to open that line of communication with the spirit within, psychedelics is another. Feed your soul with good deeds, treat others the way you want to be treated, don't cheat, steal, lie or do things that stain the soul, and your life will be easier and closer to your Heaven on Earth. This is where psychedelics bring you. They make you more aware and closer to the God within.

The soul is what is remembered of a person when the body dies. Whether that person was good or evil, the soul lives on. Strive to have a good clean soul free of evil, and you will be remembered for that goodness. Most religions believe that you will live eternally in some form of paradise when we leave our earthly body. This is why, in most religions, we should live as good a life as possible. My opinion is that an afterlife is simply the memory of one's self, by the living, after we die.

Keeping that memory alive, based on what kind of person we were while alive and how much love we had for our fellow humans, is what we will be remembered for. This might be the concept of the afterlife. Hindus and Buddhists believe they will either attain Moksha or go on to the next life. Muslims believe they will join Allah in paradise when they die. Christians believe they will join Jesus and their loved ones in Heaven. It's not clear what Jews believe happens after death. The Torah, the most holy Jewish scripture, does not talk about the afterlife but focuses on the here and now. These beliefs are part of the faith in these religions. No one knows for sure what happens when we die, so I'll keep my options open until it's my time to go. Until then, I'll try to spend my time doing good while alive.

CHAPTER 11
ANSWERS?

When asked the question, "Do you believe in God?" the questioner must define their interpretation of God before that question can be answered. There are many definitions of God, so the person being asked has to know what definition of God they are being asked about. The God that Christians believe in is different from the God that Hindus believe in, which is different from the God the Jews believe in, which is different from the God that Buddhists believe in, which is different from the God the Muslims believe in. There are as many definitions of God as there are religions, so God must first be defined before the question can be answered. The day when all the religions of the world agree on one God will be a day to celebrate peace on Earth. In my opinion, that one God is the same God of peace and love that lives in us all.

There are many unanswered questions in the spiritual and religious worlds. There are also many unanswered questions in the secular nonspiritual world. Atheists deny any existence of a God. Agnostics believe that the existence of God can't be proven. The secular community simply denies any religious or spiritual belief in God. The religious and theistic communities believe there is a God or a mystical place where peace, love, and God can be found. This place, for most religions, is Heaven or a facsimile of Heaven, for example, Utopia or Nirvana, etc. None of these beliefs of God's existence or nonexistence have true answers, only strong, dedicated believers. It is a human right to believe whatever you wish, and respecting the right of others is what is important. Those who believe in God should respect those who don't, and vice versa. Instead of arguing or trying to convince someone about God's existence, or nonexistence, you will find more peace of mind by letting people believe whatever they want.

Debating religion or politics ends up in arguments most of the time. In the early Constantine days of Christianity, if you denied Christ, you were accused of heresy and put to death. Constantine laid down the laws of Christianity, and this is when politics started creeping into the organized religion of Christianity. The Crusades, a horrific era in which Christians battled Muslims to take back land occupied by Muslims Christians previously occupied, is an example of the distance between the extremism of the church and the "word" of Jesus. Thousands of people died fighting in the name of Christianity during the Crusades. Thousands of Jews and Palestinians have died, warring for thousands of years over who should occupy Israel. Catholics and Protestants have been fighting over the occupation of Northern Ireland for years. Religious wars have been fought since the inception of religion. Killing in the name of religion shows the hypocrisy of organized religion. If a loving God exists, how can He allow death and wars to be fought in His name? How can hate and horrible death and destruction exist in the world of a peace-loving God?

These questions reinforce the nonbeliever's disbelief in a superior God. Suppose there is a God "out there", pulling the strings of life and death. In that case, He must answer for religious wars unless you believe humanity represents the mind of God and only collectively can we put an end to war and hate by tapping into the peaceful, loving God within.

If you were born and raised into a strict Catholic family, you were taught to unconditionally adhere to the ways of the church. Many Catholic people are faithful believers. If you stray from these beliefs, you will commit a sin and be strapped with guilt. This guilt would lay heavily on the young Christian's mind so that you do not stray from the Catholic doctrine for fear of "going to Hell", Hell being a place where you will suffer eternally. This blind faith is instilled in you from early on. Devout Catholics carry this fear of guilt throughout their lives.

One attribute of psychedelics is that they break you free from that guilt by opening your mind and enabling you to question the difference between the "word of Jesus" and the church dogma. It's not for me to tell anyone to go, or not to go, to church. I'm simply explaining the effect of psychedelics that helped me understand religion and spirituality apart from the churches influence. I was under the veil of Catholic guilt until my eyes and mind were opened to the true meaning of what, I believe, is what Jesus and other prophets preached. Going to church gives people a sense of feeling good about their lives, a sacrifice that earns them points in Heaven. The church, synagogue or mosque is the place to go for answers for most religious believers. I believe that the meaning of spiritual life can be found within oneself.

My inner self is where my church is, and I found that church through the psychedelic experience. The psychedelic experience allowed me to see what the prophets were preaching. I was raised as a Christian so it was easier for me to compare my pre-psychedelic Christian beliefs to my post-psychedelic Christian beliefs. I feel I have a much better understanding of what Jesus was trying to say. It's hard to explain the difference between the pre-and post-experiences. But if you understand how the cultures of the American Indian and the Mexican and Amazonian cultures commune with God through their peyote, ayahuasca and mushrooms eating ceremonies, you will understand how LSD and the like open your spiritual pathways.

I would be all for a church that was a place to go to learn the rewards of goodness without the ritual and strict adherence of the political aspects of the church of today. It could be a place to explain the rewards of doing what Christ's "word" is. A place to go for a refresher course without the rituals and rules. Many people live a Christian life without going to church. Once the knowledge of the simple teachings of Jesus, and other prophets, is known, a life of spirituality can be lived without the ritual of church. Where does the miracle and beauty of life come from? How do plants know to follow the sun across the sky? What makes animals migrate at certain times of the year? How do bees know to protect their queen? Where does the innate drive of these animals, insects and plants come from? Where does the human intellect come from? Does God make these things happen, or are these happenings what makes God? Does God make us, or do we make God? The title of this chapter is "Answers?" and there are many mysteries to which there are no answers.

To some, God is the answer to everything that happens. God is not a being sitting on a cloud, pulling the strings that control us. People speculate and pontificate and try to convince others that there are conclusive answers to these questions. It is up to the individual to answer these questions. This is the freedom of choice that is "God-given," and you'll make that choice in your mind, where your decisions, beliefs, and God are. According to the Bible, we are created in God's image. Is that image the God within? What is nature, and what is the force behind nature? Could the force that keeps these things occurring be God, or is God totally separate from nature? Flowers blooming, bees making honey, living beings reproducing, rain, wind, and all things that are considered nature are beautiful, but are they separate from the love and peace found within our hearts and minds? We recognize the beauty and power of nature, but so did the ancient civilizations who assigned a different God to each nature-producing force. Is God beyond the physical products of nature? Is God beyond the material world, or is God a part of the material world? You can believe in many Gods, as the ancients did, or you can find a single force in your life that is within you through meditation or prayer or psychedelics. When you can see and feel the connection to the insects and the plants and the animals and life of all kinds, that is when you will understand the cosmic relationship of all that is. Call it Utopia, call it Nirvana, call it nature, call it God, this, I believe, is what Jesus, Buddha, Vishnu, and all prophets tried to convey to us. Our minds, our actions, our beliefs, everything that every living thing is and does is what God is, and it is all perceived in the mind.

Understanding what these prophets understood is the paradise most spiritual people yearn for. Traveling the road to this paradise is a lifelong journey for most. But those prophets had the answer to living a peaceful, loving, tolerant understanding of life. Something in their brains connected them to this spiritual paradise beyond the material world. They may have had a psychedelic experience, or they may have been born spiritually enlightened. This Heaven, paradise, Utopia, Nirvana may never be attained by those seeking it, but the constant effort of those searching through faith is itself rewarding. Constant searching for God exercises and opens the mind to find that place where peace and love are. You don't have to believe in God to find this happiness, but those who do find this happiness believe that this is what God is. The psychedelic experience is a fast track to the connection with this beautiful place. Those who have had this enlightening experience know what I mean. Like learning to do something that you can't unlearn, for instance, reading, speaking, or riding a bicycle, you can't undo the psychedelic experience that hurls you toward the spiritual realm.

There are people born into this world who have little capacity to learn or understand, and there are people born into this world who have a great capacity to learn and be curious. There is a wide spectrum of people that humanity yields forth onto Earth. All through time, there have been people born with extraordinary minds that can solve problems or invent things previously unheard of. Socrates, Aristotle, Plato, Galileo, Archimedes, DaVinci, Newton, Einstein and many others have spectacularly advanced society. These are the geniuses of the material world. I would also include Steve Jobs in this category for inventing the mobile computer, the iPhone. Some would discount Jobs because of his use of LSD. I believe the use of LSD had a lot to do with his inventive spirit and that LSD also had a lot to do with his trips to India in his search for spiritual enlightenment. No one knows, but psychedelics could have influenced the previously mentioned geniuses. These ancient and contemporary geniuses all had a concept of God. They may not have preached about spirituality, but they all believed that there is something beyond the material world.

Buddha, Vishnu, Mohammad, Jesus, and others were the geniuses of the spiritual world. They are the people that tried to explain to the material world that the spiritual world of peace and love is what is most gratifying and how society should comport itself. They could have been born enlightened or had a psychedelic experience that enlightened them earlier in their lives. Psychedelics physically and mentally opens the doors to enlightenment by affecting parts of the brain that connects the mind and soul to the spiritual world. The brain lives in the physical world, while the mind lives in the mystical world. Thinking, understanding, comprehending, creating, emoting, and dreaming are all results of the brain-mind connection. The brain recognizes things from the physical world through the senses, and the mind interprets the messages that the brain receives.

Our eyes, ears, nose, skin, and mouth are the physical parts of the body that send messages to the brain to be interpreted into sight, hearing, smell, feel, and taste. With psychedelics, the senses become acutely enhanced. Psychedelics hold the key to the entrance of the unknown, untapped parts of the mind far from the worldly ego. It is as if you've gained a sixth sense that evolves into the spiritual realm after your psychedelic experience. You become part of a universal, cosmic, mystical, spiritual community. You will have epiphanic revelations. This is not an exaggeration. You will see and understand things from a totally different point of view. You will be a different person, far removed from the mundane world you lived in prior to the psychedelic experience. You will find yourself frequently saying, "Yes, that's right, why didn't I realize that before". From a psychedelic point of view, it is hard for me to believe that the birth of certain religions happened without some kind of psychoactive influence.

Did Buddha just decide to sit under a tree one day and search for the answers to life with no outside influence? Did Hindus decide that the energy from Shiva just happened without some kind of outside influence? Did the Last Supper include ergot-infected "manna from heaven" or "magic mushrooms"? And was the wine at the Last Supper made from a psychedelic concoction, such as psilocybin mushrooms? If these prophets weren't born with an enlightened mind, then something had to open the minds of the originators of these religions. All religions seek something beyond the material world, starting by searching within. A light that comes from somewhere and delivers the almighty message is a common theme in most religions. "The Great Spirit", "The Holy Ghost," or "Holy Spirit", "Moksha", the intangible, mystical, infinite, peaceful, loving, tolerant understanding of life are all delivered by this light, conceived in the mind. The innermost depths of the mind is where you will find "the light" or spiritual enlightenment. It doesn't come from "out there", it projects from inside your mind. This is the light all spiritual people search for.

Unconditional faith and intense dedication will bring you closer to your God. This constant dedication through prayer or meditation is what the truly faithful dedicate their lives to in order to be close to God. With psychedelics, your window to what seekers of God dedicate their entire lives will open in a twelve-hour LSD or psilocybin trip if you choose to open that window. You won't come out of the psychedelic experience immersed in spirituality, but you will, in time, see religion and God from a different, mind-expanded viewpoint.

Nobody has the real, true answers to whom, what, or where God is. Religions of all kinds believe they have the answers to these mysteries, but there are as many answers as there are religions. People seeking God will decide for themselves which spiritual path they are most comfortable with, and there are many paths to choose from, although certain paths are pre-chosen for some people. Faith in your religious belief is the key.

As we age, mature, and start to reason through perspective and wisdom, we find it easier to choose which path suits us best. But if you are born into a family with the conviction of a certain religion, you won't have a choice of what, or what not, to believe. If you stray from that religion, you'll become an outcast in your families eyes. In some countries straying from that religion will get you killed. Thankfully, in most countries, you have the choice to believe what you wish. In some countries, you have no choice. To believe there is a God, or that there is not a God, is a personal choice for most. There are places where a certain religion is demanded of its populous, and there are places where religion is taboo.

Whatever your situation is, and no matter what is demanded of you spiritually, there is one place that you and only you control and can believe whatever you wish to believe. That place is your mind. Go there and dream. Go there and believe whatever you want to believe. Go there and commune with the souls of people who no longer walk the Earth. Or go there and see if your God is there. It is your sanctuary, church, and private place where no one else can be. Many of us have found that path toward peace and love since the psychedelic experience opened our spiritual door. We are eternally thankful to have encountered our internal, personal God along the way. The connection between psychedelics and spirituality is strong but not absolute.

There are some people who have experimented with psychedelics and had no enlightening spiritual revelations. But a large majority of those who have experienced psychedelics have had their spiritual light lit. It is not a coincidence that a large part of the 1960s and 70s psychedelic generation ended up on a spiritual quest. Or that the chemists working with LSD in the 1940s and 50s dropped out of their corporate lives and turned to the spirit world after their encounters with LSD or magic mushrooms. Mind-altering substances, and their effects, have been on Earth from the beginning of time, and they may or may not have influenced religion or the search for someone or something beyond humanity. Believing there is something or someone "out there" or "within" is a personal choice.

Believing that psychedelics can answer the question of "Do you believe in God" is also a personal choice. The answer, by those who have had the psychedelic experience, that there is something beyond the material world is yes. Their use by certain cultures to commune with the spirit world is undeniable. They opened my God's eyes, and there is no harm in living a spiritual life, whether overtly or covertly, with or without the influence of the psychedelic experience.

ABOUT THE AUTHOR

John was born in the middle of the baby boom. Like many of his contemporaries, his early twenties were spent in the midst of the psychedelic years of the 1960s and 70s. He is a father, grandfather, entrepreneur, inventor, artist, and Vietnam War veteran. With this being his first book, "author" can be added to his resume.

www.ingramcontent.com/pod-product-compliance
Lightning Source LLC
Chambersburg PA
CBHW070609310726
48982CB00001B/27